The Big Test

by Elizabeth Campbell

illustrated by Marcos Calo

Saya

Doug

Kai

SERVICE · SACRIFICE · STRENGTH · SECRECY

THE ALLIANCE SERIES

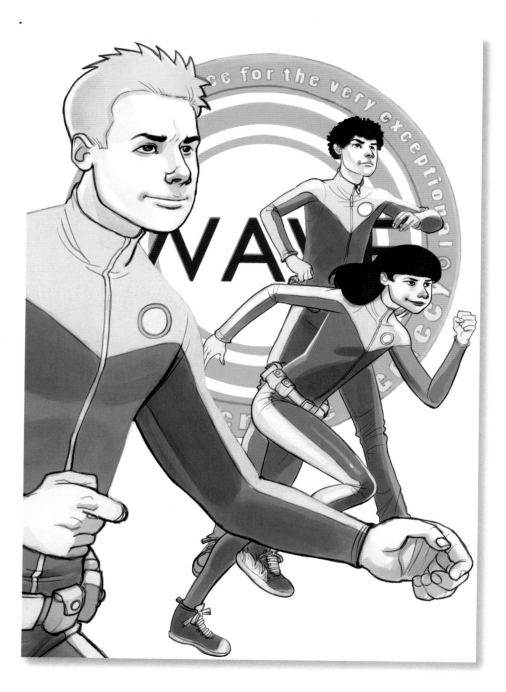

TABLE OF CONTENTS

TEST ANXIETY

I knew Friday was going to be a disaster, and not just because I expected to be blown up. That's happened before. It was because after Friday, Saya, Doug, and I—best friends for most of our lives—were probably never going to speak to each other, ever again.

We're all the kids of supers—people with super abilities—so we've always hung out together. We each have a superpower, too. Saya is fast—so fast that she needs to wear lead shoes at school to slow herself down. Doug can dig his way through anything with just his hands. I'm Kai, and I can stop time, though for only a few seconds.

Even with our abilities, we aren't supers yet, not until we pass our exams. We have to complete three levels of exams to become full-fledged members of WAVE—the Worldwide Alliance of the Very Exceptional.

But the way things were going, we'd never even pass Basic. That's why we were at each other's throats.

The Basic level is a bit boring. Sure, there's some ability and combat training, but there's also lots of rule memorization and equipment maintenance. We were dying to move up to the next level. To do that, we had to pass the exam. You get ten minutes to contain and neutralize a simulated bomb threat.

The first time through, we got blown to smithereens. We would meet for our second attempt down at WAVE headquarters on Friday night. If we failed again we'd be stuck in Basic for another whole year.

Our instructor, Dr. Hakim, told me, "Don't worry, Kai. Have faith in your team."

But the way things were going, I wasn't sure we'd still be a team after Friday.

STALE LUNCH

Saya, Doug, and I are the only WAVE members at our school. All the rest of the kids are civilians. Because of strict secrecy codes, we three pretty much just hang out with each other. It's hard to maintain friendships when you have to lie a lot to protect your true identity.

Usually, we three get along fine. But lunch on Friday was quiet. Too quiet.

Saya was picking at her food. This was ominous, because she's like a hummingbird—incredibly fast and incredibly hungry all the time. I could tell she was worried. Her mom's the head of WAVE operations; Saya didn't want to disappoint her.

Doug, on the other hand, didn't seem worried at all. He was studying a pamphlet called *Finding Your Super Self: How to Create Your Secret Identity* and jotting notes on his napkin. The pen looked like a toothpick in his shovel-sized hand.

Saya finally spoke. "I've been going over my notes." She paused. "I hope you've both been studying, too."

I nodded vaguely. Actually, I hadn't been studying. I knew the material; it just leaked out of my brain during the exam. The panic was already building in my stomach at the thought of taking it again.

"Doug?" Saya said.

He looked up. "Which do you think is a better name, Badger Boy or The Tunneling Torrent?"

"How about The Giant Dirt Bag?" Saya said. "How can you mess with that today? Especially when you failed to pack a stain stick in your utility belt last time."

"Right." Doug said. "That's soooo important. The grass stains could have killed me."

"It cost us three points."

"So what? We got blown up!"

"Those points influence our rankings!" Saya snapped. "And if you had paid attention to detail, we might not have been blown up!"

Doug fired back, "Well, your 'attention to detail' cost us a full minute while you tied the guards with regulation knots."

"If I hadn't, they might have escaped and come after us!"

"Guys," I said, trying to derail them.

Saya turned to me. "And you! We never know what you're going to do—stop time or pass out!"

That stung. Because it was true. I could freeze time for almost ten seconds, but I wasn't very reliable. The force of the chronological backwash was incredibly strong, and it could overwhelm me, especially when I was nervous. During the first attempt, I'd fainted.

"You're right," I said. "I was useless."

Saya backtracked. "Don't be stupid, Kai. You're great at stopping time in practice. Just relax."

Doug snorted. "Relax? With you carping at him?"

Saya looked at him icily. "Listen, no one in my family has ever failed this exam, and I'd better not be the first because of you!" She stalked away.

Doug went back to his pamphlet. "She's all worked up for nothing," he said. "We'll be fine."

But I knew better. We were doomed.

SYSTEM MALFUNCTION

The ready room was tense that evening. Saya was obsessively checking her utility belt. Doug was reading a comic—*MegaHero vs. The Cataclysm*. "To keep loose," he said. I was dropping a quarter over and over and trying to stop it with my mind before it hit the ground.

Only I remain unfrozen within my time bubbles. For everyone else, time seems to flow on as usual. But Saya and Doug could tell I was practicing. "Kai," Saya said, "Quit it. I don't want to wait any longer than necessary to get this over with."

"You aren't," I said. "Technically, I'm the only one who gains time." She was about to retort when Dr. Hakim arrived.

"OK, cadets," he said, "Let's look at you." We stood at attention. He took off his glasses. His golden eyes flashed over us. "Good. Your gear is in order." Dr. Hakim's super ability is x-ray vision.

"You're facing the same basic scenario," he continued. "Disable any combatants within the building, locate the bomb, and defuse it."

He replaced his glasses and looked at us intently. "Remember, you're a *team*. The whole is greater than the sum of its parts." We nodded.

"I'll be at the control board. Good luck."

We stepped through the simulator hatch. It closed, leaving us in complete darkness. A red light flickered on the wall. The air hummed with electronic activity.

A flat computer voice said, "Program launch in T minus 10...9...8...." A haze was filling my brain again, making it hard to think.

"7...6...5...."

Saya was muttering procedural codes.

"4...3...2...."

Doug cracked his knuckles. This was it.

But it wasn't it. The humming died with a whimper. We stood, tense and ready for action. Nothing.

"Dr. Hakim?" Saya called. "Hello?"

SNEAK ATTACK

There was no response. We shouted a few more times. Finally, Doug pulled the flashlight from his utility belt and opened the hatch.

The ready room was empty, its outer door ajar.

"Dr. Hakim?" Saya called. "The program malfunctioned." Silence.

"Where'd he go?" I said. "He's supposed to monitor us."

Doug moved toward the control board. There was a crunch of breaking glass. "Whoops," he said, picking up a pair of glasses. "What are these doing here?"

"Something's not right," Saya said, and then stopped as a distant burst of popping sounds echoed down the corridor.

Pulse blasters. Those weapons were illegal!

"Something's *really* not right," I said. "That's coming from the operations wing. Who's on duty?"

Saya went white. "My mom!"

Footsteps were approaching from both ends of the corridor. We pressed ourselves against the wall beside the hatch and waited.

A voice said, "Well?"

"We found two supers," another answered. "The mind reader and the x-ray guy. They're secured in the command room."

The first voice said, "Did you trigger the distress alarm?"

"Affirmative."

"Good. If we're lucky, the entire WAVE team will be here in ten minutes, and the bomb will go off with all of them inside. Now get going. Rendezvous at SPORE headquarters."

Saya, Doug, and I looked at each other in horror. *SPORE agents! Inside headquarters!* This was bad. SPORE agents were ultra-bad guys. They hated WAVE, mainly because we always stopped them from taking over the world.

Our months of training kicked in. The Alliance was in danger. Saya looked at me and mouthed, "Go!"

I felt unexpectedly calm with a real crisis to face. Gathering my energy, I pushed with my mind against the force of time. It felt like an enormous wall of water backing up around me. Everything in the world stopped except me, and in that strange, still silence, I ran into the corridor.

Four agents were frozen awkwardly in the act of running for the exit. I had ten seconds, no more. Time's weight was building every moment like a ton of water pressing against my head and ears. But I did what I could. I disarmed the men.

As I toppled back into the ready room and dropped the weapons on the floor, my bubble collapsed.

"I did it," I gasped. "Take them out."

Saya and Doug sprang into the corridor. The men turned and, of course, tried to shoot their pulse blasters. They were staring stupidly at their empty hands as Saya knocked them off their feet. Then Doug waded in. By the time I'd pulled myself together, all four bad guys were out cold. That's when we realized our mistake.

They were out cold.

And we didn't know where the bomb was.

LOCATE AND VACATE

"Doug, you hit them too hard!" said Saya.

"Kai said, 'Take them out,'" Doug said hotly. "That's what 'Take them out' means!"

"Protocol states at least one prisoner should be kept conscious for questioning," I said.

"Now you tell me."

Saya was about to lose it. She was terrified about her mom. I broke in.

"There's no time to argue. How can we locate the bomb?"

Saya said, "My mom...."

"We'll get your mom," I said. "But we've got to find the bomb. We might not be able to warn everyone before it goes off."

"No, I mean my mom reads minds. What if we carried a SPORE agent to her?"

"I'm on it," said Doug, picking up one at random. "Let's go!"

The command room was located on the other side of headquarters. As we barreled down the maze of corridors, Saya said, "How many minutes do we have?"

"Seven, maybe eight," I panted.

"I'm going ahead." She shot off like a comet.

Doug was puffing along behind. He was definitely not built for speed. "Don't talk," I said. "Just run." He grunted and picked up the pace.

Saya was untying the adults as we staggered into the command room a minute later. Dr. Hakim was unconscious, blood pooling under his right side. Saya's mom was beat up pretty badly, but alert. She knew what we needed.

Doug dropped the SPORE agent unceremoniously at her feet and ran to help Dr. Hakim. Saya's mom concentrated; then her eyes opened wide. "It's attached to the quantum generator! If that goes, it will take out half the city!"

Doug looked up from his triage kit. "That's the other side of the building again."

"…And we only have a few minutes," I said, thinking hard. "Doug, get these three out of the building. Tell any WAVE agents you meet to help clear the neighborhood. Saya, come on."

"Saya, Kai, I forbid you to go," said her mom. But Doug was already picking her up, and she was in no condition to stop us.

"It will be okay, Mom," said Saya. "Don't worry! We've got this."

UNEXPECTED VISITORS

As Saya and I took off, she repeated, "We've got this, right?"

I didn't answer directly. "You run ahead and start the disarming protocol," I said. "I'll help finish when I get there."

"Right," she said, rounding a corner. "I'll see you soon."

Instead, she stopped dead in her tracks. Three very angry looking SPORE agents were running straight toward us, their blasters drawn. We'd forgotten to tie them up.

"Oh, no," I said. They'd be on us in a moment.

"Kai," said Saya, "Do your thing. Get the weapons and keep going. I'll take care of them."

"But Saya...."

"Don't worry, Kai," she said, the light of battle in her eye. "I've got this."

There were no other options. One of us had to get through. I pulled myself together and pushed. In a moment I was running between the frozen agents, snatching their weapons and hoping a hummingbird named Saya, trained in jujitsu, was a match for three grown men.

TIMED OUT

It took all my will to keep from fainting when the time wall collapsed. I'd never done two long freezes in such quick succession. My mind and body were exhausted. I wouldn't be able to do it again.

I kept my legs stumbling through the sprawl of corridors. Finally, I reached the generator room and lurched inside, tossing the weapons into a corner. A little black box was attached to the massive generator. Its chronometer read, **:48**. *Less than a minute!* The familiar panic started to return. *I shouldn't be here! Saya's faster; Doug's stronger. I'm the one who faints.*

But you didn't, a voice said inside me. A calm voice. *And you won't now.*

My friends and my family were counting on me. The voice said again, *Not now*.

Right, I thought. *Faint later*. I drew a deep breath and pictured the textbook page on bomb disposal. *I've got this*.

I pulled the wire cutters from my utility belt. *Just follow the steps*.

The chronometer blinked 22...21...20....

Locate detonator. OK.

14...13...12....

Locate power source. Got it.

8...7...6....

Cut connection. Here goes nothing.

4...3...2....

The angry red numbers blinked and went dark. I waited for the blast, but the world remained unexploded.

I can't believe it! I thought. *We actually did it!*

And then I passed out.

RETAKES

"What?" Doug sputtered. "We've still got to take the final exam?" He stood beside Dr. Hakim's hospital bed, looking like he'd just been punched in the face.

"But we defeated SPORE agents!" said Saya. "We defused a bomb. We rescued you! WAVE gave us medals!"

Saya actually *had* been punched in the face. She had stitches on her lower lip and a black eye, but, as her mom kept saying proudly, "You should have seen the other guys."

Dr. Hakim was apologetic. "Believe me, I'm grateful, Doug. Your quick action saved my life. But it's out of my hands. Cadets *must* pass the standard exam." We stared at him, dumbfounded.

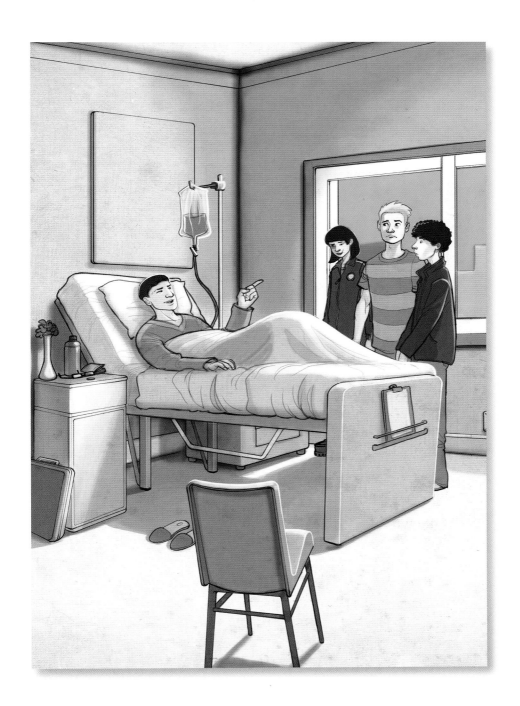

"And anyway," he continued with a grin, "You wouldn't want to be *scored* on Friday's events. Rendering prisoners unconscious, leaving enemy agents and their weapons unsecured, flouting a direct order? Not to mention destroying a superior's valuable eyewear!"

Saya started to smile, but stopped. Her mouth probably hurt too much.

"Honestly," Dr. Hakim said, "even Kai can't worry about failing now, can he?"

I grinned back. "No, I can't." I looked at Saya and Doug. "I know my team, sir, and I have faith in us all."